PUFFIN BOOKS

SECRET SANTA

Opposites . . .

Black . . . White
Ugly . . . Beautiful
Hot . . . Cold
North . . . South
Dog . . . Brussel sprout

Hang on a sec, let me explain that last one.

I love Christmas. Because, basically I'm just a big kid! The whole prezzies, food and Christmas telly thing is just brilliant. You see, lots of things are *just for Christmas*. Nice things like decorations, crimbo trees, turkey lurkey, mistletoe, silly paper hats, Quality Street and new socks. And some horrid things, like Brussel sprouts, parsnips and trying to look pleased when you open the new socks! But we do these things because they're *just for Christmas*.

I was driving home the other day and I saw a sticker on the car in front. It read, 'Dogs are for life, not just for Christmas.' So that makes my dog Lara the exact opposite of a Brussel sprout. How fab is that!

Happy Christmas from Andrew and Lara

*Books by Andrew Cope*

Spy Dog
Spy Dog Captured!
Spy Dog Unleashed!
Spy Dog Superbrain
Spy Dog Rocket Rider
Spy Dog Secret Santa
Spy Dog Teacher's Pet
Spy Dog Rollercoaster!

Spy Pups Treasure Quest
Spy Pups Prison Break
Spy Pups Circus Act
Spy Pups Danger Island
Spy Pups Survival Camp
Spy Pups Training School

Spy Dog Joke Book

# SPY DOG
## SECRET SANTA

ANDREW COPE

*Illustrated by James de la Rue*

PUFFIN

PUFFIN BOOKS

Published by the Penguin Group
Penguin Books Ltd, 80 Strand, London WC2R ORL, England
Penguin Group (USA) Inc., 375 Hudson Street, New York, New York 10014, USA
Penguin Group (Canada), 90 Eglinton Avenue East, Suite 700, Toronto, Ontario, Canada M4P 2Y3
(a division of Pearson Penguin Canada Inc.)
Penguin Ireland, 25 St Stephen's Green, Dublin 2, Ireland (a division of Penguin Books Ltd)
Penguin Group (Australia), 707 Collins Street, Melbourne, Victoria 3008, Australia
(a division of Pearson Australia Group Pty Ltd)
Penguin Books India Pvt Ltd, 11 Community Centre, Panchsheel Park, New Delhi – 110 017, India
Penguin Group (NZ), 67 Apollo Drive, Rosedale, Auckland 0632, New Zealand
(a division of Pearson New Zealand Ltd)
Penguin Books (South Africa) (Pty) Ltd, Block D, Rosebank Office Park, 181 Jan Smuts Avenue,
Parktown North, Gauteng 2193, South Africa

Penguin Books Ltd, Registered Offices: 80 Strand, London WC2R ORL, England

puffinbooks.com

First published 2010
This edition published 2012
001

Text copyright © Andrew Cope and Stella Maidment, 2010
Illustrations copyright © James de la Rue, 2010
All rights reserved

The moral right of the author and illustrator has been asserted

Set in Bembo
Typeset by Palimpsest Book Production Limited, Falkirk, Stirlingshire
Printed in Great Britain by Clays Ltd, St Ives plc

British Library Cataloguing in Publication Data
A CIP catalogue record for this book is available from the British Library

ISBN: 978-0-141-34558-1

www.greenpenguin.co.uk

MIX
Paper from
responsible sources
FSC™ C018179
www.fsc.org

Penguin Books is committed to a sustainable
future for our business, our readers and our planet.
This book is made from Forest Stewardship
Council™ certified paper.

ALWAYS LEARNING　　　　　**PEARSON**

*To anyone who has a pet. Make sure you love your pet and give them a special hug this Christmas (unless you've got a fish or a porcupine).*

# Contents

## 1. Lights and Darkness

The shadowy figures stood together in the darkness, their hands pushed deep into their pockets to keep them warm. Tall and short, young and old, their bodies bundled shapelessly in thick winter clothes. A few had torches, sending beams of eerie light upwards on to their faces. They formed a semicircle on the frosty grass, all staring silently in the same direction.

Under a single spotlight, a boy of about twelve scrambled on to a makeshift stage and stood in front of a microphone. He was followed by his sister, just a little younger, who turned and helped a much younger brother up to join them.

'Welcome to the annual ceremony of the turning on of the village Christmas lights!'

said Ben, the older boy, raising his voice slightly even though the microphone amplified his words. 'As you know, we always invite a special person to perform this important task and this year it's our very own local celebrity. I wonder if you can guess who she is?' Ben beamed at the assembled crowd. 'Well, here's a clue: she's a brilliant and highly trained Secret Service agent; she can defuse bombs, crack codes, understand at least twelve languages –'

'And she's caught way more baddies than I've had Christmas dinners!' interrupted Ben's younger brother, jumping up and grabbing the microphone.

'Thank you, Ollie,' frowned Ben, easing the microphone away from his brother. 'She's the head of our neighbourhood watch, and a mother of seven – two of them are here tonight . . .'

At this point there was an excited *Woof! Woof!* from a small black puppy at the front of the crowd and everyone laughed.

'And thank you, Spud!' said Ben, as the young dog jumped excitedly up towards the stage. 'But most of all,' he went on, 'she's a very important part of my family. Please welcome Secret Agent GM451 – or as we all know her, LARA!'

Gloved hands joined in muffled applause. Several of the smaller, four-legged members barked and meowed as a black-and-white dog about the size of a Labrador, with one ear sticking up and one ear flopping down, bounded up on to the stage.

Lara stood for a moment looking down at the shadowy faces of her friends and neighbours. All her animal neighbourhood watch group were there – except George the tortoise, who always spent Christmas in a cardboard box under the stairs.

In the front row were her two lively pups, Spud and his sister Star, fidgeting about beside their handsome black pedigree dad. Next to them were some of her adopted family – Mr and Mrs Cook and Gran, who lived opposite; and of course the children were on the stage beside her – Lara's very best friends, Ben, Sophie and little Ollie.

At times like these Lara couldn't help thinking that things might have been very different if she'd carried on with her early life as a Spy Dog – or worse still, if the bullet that had left a permanent hole in her right ear had been fired just a little lower. That was a terrible mission. She had been forced to go undercover and pretend to be a normal dog. The Cook family had come to the RSPCA rescue centre looking for an ordinary pet, but Lara had selected them as her future family – and the children had soon realized that she was anything but ordinary . . .

*No*, thought Lara, *I'm glad I'm just a retired Spy Dog now.* She felt pleased and proud to be part of such a happy, friendly community. *And Christmas is my favourite time. Star and Spud have already put up their Christmas stockings. They're so excited about Santa!*

'Go on, Lara. What are you waiting for? Turn on the lights!' whispered Ben.

*What am I doing?* thought Lara, giving herself a little shake. *I've only got one mission this evening and it's an easy one too. I'd better get on with it!*

She stood on her hind legs and winked at Ben. He addressed the microphone and counted the crowd down from ten. Lara waited for the right moment before turning the switch with her paw. Hundreds of light bulbs sprang into life along the houses around the village green, and in the middle of the grass a huge Christmas tree could suddenly be seen covered in tiny coloured stars, twinkling brightly into the night, lighting up the faces of the crowd as they cheered and clapped and whistled.

*This is the life for me!* thought Lara as she and the children jumped down from the stage, and the crowd moved off towards the village hall where bowls of hot punch and mince pies were waiting.

Suddenly, a shiny black four-by-four came

screaming down the hill into the village, stopping everyone in their tracks with the sound of its powerful engine. Its tyres screeched as it skidded around the bend beside the pond, then, finding its balance again, it carried on driving straight towards them.

*Surely the driver's going to stop*, thought Lara. *He can see there's a crowd of people in the road.*

But the car just kept on going. As the people started to scatter, Lara's training kicked in. *Make sure the children are safe.* The pups had already scampered to the other side of the road and were waiting there with Mum and Dad, but Ollie and Sophie were just beginning to cross. When they heard the car they hesitated for a second. It was just enough time for Lara to hurl herself in front of them and give them each a really hard push in the chest with her front paws. They tumbled backwards on to the village green and landed in a tangled heap.

Then Lara looked around for Ben. He had started to run but had tripped over Felix the tabby cat, who bolted under his feet. Everyone else was across the road but Ben was lying flat on his face – right in the path of the car!

Lara didn't stop to think. She leapt into the road and grabbed the seat of Ben's trousers in her teeth. Then she pulled him on to his feet and, remembering her best judo move, used Ben's own weight against him to hurl him to the side of the road.

Ben was safe but Lara was still in the path of the speeding car. It was almost on her now. There was no time to run. Lara could see the sickly pale face and squinty blue eyes of the driver and she could tell he had no intention of stopping. Instead he just put his hand on the horn and kept it there . . . The noise was deafening.

From the roadside Lara heard Sophie scream and Star give a piercing, frightened yelp. A thought shot through her mind – *Are these the last sounds I am ever going to hear?*

But a Spy Dog never gives up. *I've got it!* Lara took a flying leap into the air. Reaching upwards, she just managed to hook her front paws over the branch of an overhanging tree. As the speeding car shot underneath, she clung on, swinging perilously, the claws of her back feet scraping the car's roof.

It was over in seconds. The car had gone and

Lara lost her balance and tumbled to the ground, doing her best to look casual. *It's all in a day's work for a Licensed Assault and Rescue Animal, you know. They didn't call me L.A.R.A for nothing!*

Spud and Star ran to their mum for a hug. 'Who was that nasty driver?' woofed Star.

Then everyone started talking at once.

'What a maniac!'

'Someone could have been killed!'

'Did you get his number?'

'No, he was going too fast.'

Dad rushed up to Lara. 'Lara, I think you just saved Ben's life!'

'Yes, er, thanks, Lara,' said Ben, sounding grateful but embarrassed. Lara had accidentally ripped a huge hole in the seat of his new cargo trousers and some of the girls from school were waiting on the other side of the road. 'Mum, I think I'll just go back to the house for a minute. Is that OK?'

Lara shooed the pups off towards the village hall where she knew there would be mince pies. She decided to walk with Ben. Her legs were shaky. *That was too close for comfort*, she thought. *Action and adventure seem to follow me around. I just want a quiet retirement. And a peaceful Christmas.*

'Why is Ben walking backwards?' asked Ollie loudly.

'Never mind, Ollie,' smiled Mum. 'Let's go and have a mince pie.'

## 2. Carol Singing

'Postman! Postman!' Star and Spud raced to the letterbox as a stream of envelopes poured down on to the hall floor. 'I like Christmas!' woofed Spud. 'Look at all these cards!'

The children were just finishing breakfast when the two pups trotted in, each carrying a small pile of post carefully in their mouths.

'Thank you!' said Sophie. 'Oh, look! This one's from Professor Cortex. I recognize his tiny writing.' She opened the card and read out the message inside:

Happy Christmas to all the Cook family, and especially to Agent GM451 and the Spy Pups,
Best wishes,
Maximus Cortex
PS I will be in London on Friday for a meeting. Would you join me afterwards for a trip to the pantomime? You can stay the night in one of the Secret Service visitors' flats overlooking the river.

'Wow!' said Ben, putting his cereal bowl into the dishwasher. 'That would be great!'

'Do you think Lara and the pups can come too?' asked Ollie through a mouthful of toast. Ollie was especially fond of Spud and Star because they were the little ones – a bit like him.

*I'm sure the professor would want me there,* thought Lara. *After all he was the one who trained me as a Spy Dog in the first place — but I think the pups might be a bit too young.*

'We'll have to ask Mum,' said Sophie, picking up her backpack. 'Hurry up, Ollie, it's a fun day today — the last day of the school term and then carol singing round the village this evening!' Carol singing was another village tradition. Every year all the children in the neighbourhood went from house to house singing carols and collecting money for charity.

That night they were helped by Lara on the mouth organ and some enthusiastic howling from Spud and Star. *I must teach them to read music soon*, thought Lara. *I think Spud would be a natural on the trumpet.*

Like their mum, the pups were highly intelligent and Lara had agreed that the professor could put them on his special accelerated learning programme — the same one she had followed as a young dog. They were already officially Spy Pups and they were keen to learn as many skills as they could as they both really wanted to be proper secret agents when they grew up.

★

It was another cold night and by the time the carol singers had sung their way up and down the old part of the village and into the new estate, their hands and feet were frozen – but their collection box felt satisfyingly full.

Everyone loved the carols and as the children made their way along the streets, front doors opened one by one as people came out to listen and add their contributions to the box.

But when the singers got to old Mrs Perkins's house they were surprised to find that her front door stayed firmly closed.

'Perhaps she didn't hear the doorbell,' said Sophie, ringing it again. 'Or maybe she just doesn't want to come out in the cold.'

'But Mrs Perkins always comes out!' protested Ollie. 'She usually gives us a chocolate biscuit too!'

*A biscuit?* Spud's ears pricked up. *Ring that bell again!*

'Never mind, Ollie,' laughed Ben. 'Come on, let's keep going, everyone. We've almost finished now.'

But Lara wasn't happy. *I think I'll just nip round the back and investigate.* She put her mouth organ on the ground and trotted off down the side of the house.

'What are you doing, Lara?' called Ben. 'There are loads of reasons why Mrs Perkins might not want to open her door tonight. It's not polite to march all round her garden!'

Lara shook her head. *Something isn't right*, she thought. *Now let me see: all the lights downstairs are on, front and back, but the curtains are closed – I can't see in. No lights on upstairs, curtains open. No. She can't have gone to bed.*

Lara woofed loudly and banged her paw on the kitchen window. Then she listened hard. She could just hear the sound of angry voices arguing inside. Her hackles went up and she growled despite herself. Then she realized that she knew the voices well.

*It's just* EastEnders *on the telly! It sounds exciting, though. Maybe Mrs P is watching it and doesn't want to be disturbed.* Then she heard something else. Was it another voice? Could it be someone calling? She strained her ears, trying to separate the sounds, but it was just too hard to tell. *I can't afford to take the chance*, thought Lara. *I may be just a family pet these days but I still know when something doesn't quite add up. I've got to check that Mrs P's OK.*

Looking up, Lara noticed that the very top of the upstairs bedroom window was open. It was a tiny gap, far too narrow for a person to squeeze through, too small for a dog like Lara too.

*This is a case for the animal neighbourhood watch!* thought Lara as she raced round to the front of

the house where the pups and the carol singers were waiting.

Since Lara had been living with the Cooks she had transformed a group of ordinary local pets into a specialist neighbourhood-watch unit. They met regularly for training and exercises and were proud of the way they kept their village free from crime. Star and Spud weren't part of the team yet but Lara had already taught them the emergency call.

'OK, you two,' said Lara to the pups. 'On my signal – go!' Suddenly, the street was filled with noise, not the musical sound of Christmas carols but the sound of three dogs howling loudly, in a special pattern too: one long howl, one bark, then another long howl. It was the call to action!

## 3. Watch Out!

Scottie in the next street heard it first and joined in too. Then Patch, who lived on the corner and had the loudest bark in the neighbourhood, added his deep voice to the call. Both of them came running out to help. Within minutes the whole team had assembled in Mrs Perkins's front garden.

'This is ridiculous,' said Ben. 'Lara, you're overreacting!'

But Lara took no notice. 'I need a volunteer,' she barked. 'Someone brave and agile, with an excellent head for heights.'

Maggie the black-and-white cat stepped forward straight away. She stood on her hind legs and puffed out her chest like she'd seen Lara do. 'At your service,' she saluted.

'OK, come with me,' said Lara. Everyone

followed as she led Maggie to the back of the house and showed her the window. The cat understood immediately what she had to do.

With one bound Maggie leapt on to the trunk of a nearby tree, digging her claws firmly into the bark. She'd climbed trees before, but never one as tall as this. Higher and higher she went until she was level with Mrs Perkins's upstairs window. Then she began to make her way cautiously along a branch towards the house. She looked down and immediately wished she hadn't. She was reassured by remembering that cats have nine lives.

'Be careful, girl,' called Felix from below. 'That branch gets thin towards the end. It might not hold your weight.'

'Don't worry! I'll be OK,' replied Maggie bravely.

Everyone gasped as Maggie suddenly lost her footing and started to fall. Her claws extended and she scrambled for a hold as she saw one of her lives slipping away. She crashed through some leaves before her claws finally dug into a branch and she hung, back legs kicking, while beneath her the children and animals held their breath. Like a skilful acrobat, Maggie somersaulted round and managed to swing herself back on to a thicker branch. There was a collective sigh of relief from below. The brave cat was soon edging slowly back along the branch towards the window.

*Now for the tricky bit*, breathed Lara.

As Maggie reached the end of the branch it began to buckle under her weight. She leapt for the open window and just managed to hook her front paws over the edge. *Another life gone!* In the blink of an eye she had slithered through the gap and was in.

Star punched the air in delight.

Everyone waited. *I hope Mrs Perkins likes cats*, thought Spud. *She might get a shock if she suddenly sees one coming down her stairs!*

A minute later Maggie's face appeared at the window. 'Call an ambulance!' she miaowed urgently. 'Mrs Perkins has fallen and hurt her leg!'

Lara couldn't speak Cat but she could understand it. She turned to Ben and pointed to the mobile phone in his pocket, but Ben had already got the message.

'OK, Lara,' he said. 'I'm really sorry I doubted you. I'll ring for help.'

When the ambulance came, the paramedics found Mrs Perkins lying on the kitchen floor with Maggie sitting close beside her. 'I was in such a hurry to hear the carols I slipped and fell over,' she said. 'I couldn't move. I'm so glad this little one came and found me!'

'Will she be OK?' asked Sophie, as Mrs Perkins was carried into the ambulance.

'Yes, love,' said the paramedic. 'It's not too bad. She'll be home in time for Christmas. Lucky you raised the alarm, though. She could have been there for some time.'

'It's Lara we have to thank for that,' said Ben, giving Lara a pat. 'And Maggie, too, of course.'

## 4. Merry Christmas, Mr Strange

'Do we need to carry on up to End House?' asked Sophie once all the excitement was over and the neighbourhood-watch team had scampered home. 'Is anyone living there now?'

End House was the very last house in the village, down a long, dark drive with tall trees on either side. Its owner lived abroad but rented it out from time to time. No one ever seemed to stay there long.

'There is someone there – just for a few weeks,' said Jamie, whose dad ran the village store. 'He's called Stanley Strange – and he *is* strange too! I think he's some kind of computer geek – he bought all the computer magazines in the shop.'

'That's not strange!' protested Ollie, who loved his computer games. 'That's really cool. Come on, guys, we can't leave him out!'

So the children and Lara made their way down the shadowy drive with Spud and Star running ahead of them. The house was in total darkness except for one room on the ground floor illuminated only by the pale light of a laptop computer. They could see a thin figure hunched over the screen, staring at it intently, his long fingers tapping furiously on the keyboard.

*That man looks familiar*, thought Lara. *Where have I seen him before?*

'I'll count you in, Lara!' said Ben, interrupting her thoughts. 'We'll do "Silent Night". One, two, three . . .'

*That's my favourite!* Lara began to blow on the mouth organ and the children joined in, softly at first and then slightly louder, their voices blending perfectly. *It sounds beautiful – even though I say it myself*, thought Lara.

Unfortunately, Stanley Strange didn't agree. As soon as the carol began, he started away from his screen and looked quickly from left to right. Then he slammed the laptop closed, leapt to his feet and raced to the window. Stanley saw the smiling faces of the children and Ollie giving him a friendly wave. He opened the window and shouted, 'Stop that awful noise! Go away! This is private property!'

Lara stopped playing abruptly and the carol singers' voices faded to silence.

'We've just come to wish you a merry Christmas, Mr Strange,' said one of the boys politely. 'We're collecting for a children's charity.'

'Well, you can forget about that for a start!' hissed Stanley. 'I'm not giving you any money. I hate Christmas and I hate, hate, HATE children. Understand? Now get out of here before I lose my temper! Go on – scram!'

Spud began to growl and Star looked at Lara questioningly. 'Is he threatening the children? Shall we bite him?'

'No. We should take the children home,' woofed Lara, turning quickly away.

It was then that Spud noticed a black four-wheel drive parked at the side of the house.

'Hey, look, Mum! Isn't that the car that nearly ran us over the other night?'

'So *that's* where I've seen him before,' said Lara. 'That explains a lot. Come on, pups, let's get out of here.'

As Lara and the children hurried away Spud whispered to his sister. 'I've got an idea! Let's jump on his car with our muddy paws!'

Before Star could answer, Spud leapt on to

the bonnet and marched backwards and forwards leaving dirty paw marks all over the paintwork and the windscreen.

'Serves him right!' giggled Star as she bounded up on to the roof to add her own prints — but then she stopped suddenly. 'Spud! Spud! Look inside the car!'

Star stared in amazement at a pile of clothes lying neatly on the back seat. 'Look! Red trousers and a red coat, a black belt and big black boots, a hat with a white fur trim — and yes, there it is — a white false beard. Do you know what that is?

'Of course I do, silly!' said Spud. 'It's a Father Christmas outfit!'

The pups looked at each other in excitement, sensing the beginning of a mystery. 'The question is,' said Star, 'if he hates Christmas and children so much, what's a Father Christmas outfit doing in Stanley Strange's car?'

## 5. Page Forty-three

'There may be a perfectly innocent explanation,' said Lara firmly the next day. 'I agree it's a bit surprising for a man like Stanley Strange to have a Santa outfit, but it isn't against the law! And by the way, I don't approve of you two climbing all over his car like that. Just because he was rude to us doesn't mean you have to behave badly too.'

Spud and Star hung their heads. 'Yes, Mum. Sorry, Mum,' they muttered.

'Now, I'm going to London today with the family and you'll be staying here with Gran, so I want best behaviour from both of you, please. We'll be back tomorrow afternoon. I hope you can stay out of mischief till then!'

The children's gran often looked after the pups and her house was a home from home for them. 'I'm making sausage rolls,' she said kindly. 'You can help me if you like. You never know, there might be a few spare ones for you to try!'

That was enough for Spud. He loved his food, and Star always liked staying at Gran's because she had a great collection of jigsaws. They waved the family off and followed Gran happily into her kitchen.

The Cook family and Lara travelled by train to London and then made their way to the MI6 offices where the professor was having his meeting.

'Wow, it's amazing!' gasped Ben, staring up at the huge green-and-white building with its rows of windows overlooking the river. 'It looks like a cross between a castle and an ocean liner.'

Right on time Professor Cortex came hurrying out of the main door to greet them. He was looking unusually festive in a red bow tie.

'So this is where it all happens?' said Mum. 'The headquarters of the Secret Service!'

'It's not very secret, is it?' snorted Ollie, who

always spoke his mind. 'Not if everyone knows where it is.'

'I suppose not,' answered the professor, smiling, 'although no one knows what happens inside — and, of course, there could be other places too . . .'

Just then a car with blacked-out windows stopped beside them, leaving its engine running.

The professor passed Ben a copy of a London guidebook, saying loudly, 'Well, it was very nice to see you all.' He added in an undertone, 'I think you might find page forty-three particularly interesting, Ben'. Then he opened the door, climbed into the back seat and the car disappeared into the traffic.

'What's going on?' said Ollie. 'I thought we were going to the pantomime!'

Ben turned hastily to page forty-three. A piece of paper had been pasted into the book with a map and some special instructions for him to follow. Ben's eyes shone with excitement. 'Spy stuff! This is going to be fun!' He studied the map for a few seconds. 'OK, everyone, follow me,' said Ben as, with Lara beside him, he led Mr and Mrs Cook, Sophie and Ollie away from the river, under a bridge and into a quiet side street where there was a long row of terraced houses. Glancing at the book again, Ben went up to one of the doors and rang the bell.

A plump, middle-aged woman in a pink cardigan opened the door and immediately threw her arms round Ben.

Ben looked at the note in the book once more. 'Auntie Marion!' said Ben, his voice a bit smothered in the hug. 'I've brought the family to see you.'

'You're very welcome,' said the woman. 'Come in, come in, I'll put the kettle on.'

*I recognize 'Auntie Marion' from the old days,* thought Lara, *She's a brilliant doctor of physics – specializing in laser technology.* But Lara knew better than to react in any way. *I'm just an ordinary family pet on an ordinary family visit,* she said to herself. *After all, you never know who might be watching.*

They all went into the house. A flight of stairs led up in front of them and a small front room led off to one side. The television was on and a fat tabby cat was snoozing beside a tinsel Christmas tree.

'Is she our auntie, Dad?' said Ollie, who was understandably confused. 'Why haven't you told us about her?'

'Never seen her before in my life!' chuckled Dad. Then he pointed to Ben's guidebook and gave Ollie a wink. 'Spy stuff,' he mouthed.

'Erm, Auntie . . .' said Ben, glancing again at page forty-three. 'I wonder if Ollie could use your toilet?'

'But I don't . . .' started Ollie, who was still finding it hard to understand what was going on.

'Sssh, Ollie,' hissed Sophie. 'Yes, you do!'

'It's in here,' said the woman, opening a door under the stairs. 'I've just had it redecorated. Why don't you all have a look?'

Sophie and Ben couldn't help giggling as all the family, including Lara, piled into a very tiny downstairs toilet. It was a bit of a squash to say the least, especially when 'Auntie Marion' shut the door firmly on them from the outside.

'What happens now?' whispered Sophie.

Ben pulled the chain and, as the sound of running water filled their ears, so the whole room started to sink, slowly and smoothly downwards. It stopped gently, the door opened and there was the professor, smiling.

## 6. A Secret Weapon

'Hello again!' laughed the professor. 'Well done, Ben, you followed my instructions perfectly. Now, I want to show you why I came to London today.'

They were in a huge basement that must have stretched underneath all the houses in the street. Everything was bright white and brilliantly lit. There were laboratories, offices and even, far in the distance, a swimming pool and a gym. It was clear that many people usually worked there, yet the whole area was almost entirely empty. *It's getting late*, thought Lara. *Everyone's gone home for the Christmas holidays.*

At the far end of the laboratory, a last assistant was hanging up his white coat and putting on his anorak, but in another section nearby, four

bright-looking dogs were still working hard at their computers.

'These are the latest batch of animal agents,' explained the professor. 'They'll all be on duty over Christmas, of course. In fact Agent CV89 is just off now, aren't you?'

A Welsh springer spaniel with brown ears and freckles on his nose got up, wagged his tail at the family and hurried towards the lift.

'Good luck!' called Lara. *He's very young*, she thought. *This must be his first mission.*

'Thanks, I'm going to need it!' woofed the spaniel with a smile.

'Now,' said the professor. 'I'm very pleased with my latest invention. In fact, I've just been showing it to my bosses at M16 today and I have to say they were impressed.'

He opened his briefcase and took out a small plastic bag containing a single bright blue ball, about the size of a marble. He put the bag carefully into the palm of Sophie's hand.

'A gobstopper?'

'Not exactly, young lady. Think of it more as a baddie stopper. You are now in possession of something the Secret Service has been trying to create for years – a totally non-violent weapon. It can stop baddies in their tracks in an instant without hurting them at all.'

'But how?' asked Sophie. She knew the professor was clever but this seemed too good to be true.

'It's made from an extremely powerful chemical that affects the human brain,' replied the professor. 'At the moment it's inactive but if this 'bullet' is fired from a gun and hits someone at speed, it will explode on impact. One whiff of the gas it gives off and the victim

immediately gets the giggles. Then he starts to
laugh, and within a fraction of a second he's
entirely helpless. He can't move, he can't think.

He's incapacitated! All he can do is laugh. It's extremely effective.'

'That's brilliant,' said Mum, 'and are you sure it's harmless?'

'No side effects whatsoever,' said the professor proudly. 'That's the beauty of it. This is the prototype. Now it's been approved by my bosses it can go straight into production. Our agents will be issued with guns loaded with these secret weapons by the end of January.'

He nodded kindly at Sophie. 'You can keep that one as a souvenir if you like – but don't go showing it to any enemy agents!'

'Wow! Thank you.' Sophie put the bag carefully in her rucksack. 'This is a little bit of history!'

'And now,' said the professor, smiling, 'I think we've got time for a pizza before we go on to the theatre. I don't know about you but I'm starving!'

Everybody loved the pantomime. The professor had got them a private box, so Lara could sit in the shadows and not be noticed. The children enjoyed hanging over the edge and looking sideways at the stage. There was lots of shouting and singing and throwing sweets into the audience but most of all there was lots and lots of laughing.

'No need for the professor's secret weapon here tonight!' said Dad.

That night the Cook family stayed in an ultra-modern flat with floor-to-ceiling windows overlooking the River Thames. It only had one bedroom so the children slept on sofas in the living room but that was fun too.

Lara sat up late looking at the reflections on the water. She thought of Star and Spud fast asleep at Gran's. *It's been a lovely day. I wish they could have been here too*, she thought. *I hope they're keeping out of trouble while I'm away.*

She didn't know that, at that very minute, the pups were planning an adventure that could get them into very serious trouble indeed.

## 7. The Pups' Mission

'There's definitely something funny going on up at End House,' whispered Spud, as the two pups lay in their baskets in Gran's cosy kitchen, 'and, as Spy Pups, I think it's our duty to investigate.'

'I agree,' whispered Star. 'We need more information. Maybe there *is* an innocent explanation, like Mum said; if so, we'll find out what it is.'

'In that case we need a plan,' said Spud sleepily. 'Every mission needs a proper plan . . .'

There was a short silence while both puppies thought hard. Then Star had an idea. 'Remember that tracking device the professor gave us to practise with? We could go back now and fix it on Strange's car while he's asleep.'

Spud yawned. His tummy was full of sausage

rolls. It was past his usual bedtime and his blanket was just getting nice and warm. 'Mmm, or we could go tomorrow morning – really early before anyone is awake.'

'Oooh yes! A dawn raid!' said Star. 'I've seen them do that on the telly! But we won't have to break down any doors, or do anything dangerous, will we, Spud? *Spud?*'

Her only reply was a little snuffly snore.

At five o'clock the next morning, the two pups, armed with a tiny tracking device, were creeping up the drive towards Stanley Strange's house. 'Don't walk on the gravel, Spud,' whispered Star. 'It's too crunchy. Follow me along the edge where there's grass.' Star scampered ahead, springing lightly. Spud lolloped behind, his tummy swinging heavily.

It was completely dark and didn't feel like morning at all. Heavy clouds covered the moon, and one or two snowflakes flew about in the wind.

'Look, Star! Snow! Wow! Do you think we'll have snow for Christmas? Wouldn't that be great!' Spud went cross-eyed as he examined a snowflake that had landed on his nose.

'Concentrate on the mission, Spud,' said Star strictly. 'There's the car. Now, let's see if the Santa outfit is still inside.'

The pups jumped on the bonnet and tried to peer through the car's windows but this time it was too dark to see. *I wonder if we could pick the lock*, thought Star. *But what if the car's got an alarm?*

She looked for a winking light on the dashboard. 'Hey, wait a minute!' she said.

'I think he's forgotten to lock it!' She went round to the back door, leapt up and pushed hard against the handle. Sure enough, the door swung open and the car's interior lights came on.

'Great!' said Spud, jumping in. 'Now we can have a proper look.'

The hat, the boots and the white beard were still lying on the back seat but the rest of the outfit had gone. Something else had been added instead – a sack packed with objects of different shapes and sizes.

'It's filled with presents!' said Spud excitedly. 'Toys, I bet! Maybe we've got it wrong and Stanley Strange is nicer than we thought. I wonder if there's a pirate ship in there? Or a racing car? Or maybe some choccies?'

Spud burrowed into the sack until only his short, plump back legs and his wagging tail could be seen poking out of the end.

'Well,' Spud's voice sounded disappointed in the depths of the sack. 'There are a lot of boxes wrapped in Christmas paper, but they all feel really light. I think they're fake presents, not real ones . . .'

'Is that all?' asked Star from the outside, addressing Spud's tail.

'No, there are some other things too – a giant box of matches and – *yikes!* A rope . . . and a blindfold and . . . and . . . a big heavy baseball bat.' Spud began to wriggle backwards. 'I don't like this, Star. Let's get out of here!'

Just then Star heard the sound of footsteps crunching across the gravel from the direction of the house.

'*Spud!*' she squeaked. 'It's Strange. He's coming this way!'

Spud's rear end scuttled straight back into the sack. 'Shut the door quickly and hide in here with me,' he hissed. 'Hurry! That man is dangerous!'

In the nick of time, Star pulled the car door gently closed and slithered into the sack. The two pups huddled together, trying to keep perfectly still as the footsteps drew nearer and Strange climbed into the driver's seat. He was talking quietly into his mobile phone.

'OK, you've got the name of the shop, haven't you?' said Strange in his thin, whiny voice. 'Yes, that's right, the big department store in London.'

*He's planning something – I knew it!* thought Spud. *We'd better listen carefully.*

Strange went on, 'Why today? Because it's the biggest shopping day in the biggest shopping week of the year, that's why! All those mummies and daddies buying expensive

Christmas presents for their nasty little sprogs. The shop will have taken millions. It's the perfect day for a robbery.'

*A robbery! He's planning to rob a big London store!* Spud fought to control his wagging tail.

Then Strange laughed. It wasn't a nice laugh, either. *More of a snigger*, thought Star.

'Don't worry. All I need is a few minutes on one of the store's computers and I can move all the money out of the shop's bank account and

straight into ours . . . Yes, all of it! No, of course they won't be able to trace it! What do you think I've been working on all these weeks? I can guarantee no one will ever know how – or where – the money went. It's the perfect crime! But you have to do your bit too . . . OK . . . Twelve o'clock, midday . . . Right. See you!'

Then Stanley Strange, looking unusually plump in his jolly red, padded Santa outfit, drove off through the sleeping village, along the empty roads and out towards the motorway.

## 8. Santa's Grotto

It was a long way to London. Strange drove fast and very badly, hurling the car about like a tiny boat on a stormy sea. Star felt travel-sick for most of the way and was glad she hadn't eaten any breakfast. Spud felt tired but didn't dare fall asleep.

After a while the sun rose and a pale, watery light filled the car, but it was still as dark as night for the pups in the bottom of the sack.

Eventually the car slowed, and soon it was stopping and starting, crawling through heavy traffic. They were off the motorway and on their way to the centre of London.

*But what do we do then?* thought Spud anxiously. *What happens when Strange opens the sack and finds us?*

Finally the car stopped and Strange got out

of the driver's seat and opened the back door. The pups tensed their muscles, hardly daring to breathe. Strange sat down and put on the black boots, then he picked up the hat and beard and put them on too, admiring himself in the car's wing mirror.

'Ho! Ho! Ho!' he said, in a rather poor attempt to sound like Father Christmas. 'Soon I'll be a multi-millionaire!'

*Not if we can help it*, thought Star.

Finally, Strange picked up the sack and swung it awkwardly over his shoulder. The pups tumbled from left to right inside.

'Funny, it feels heavier than I thought,' muttered Strange. 'Oh well, not far to go.'

He marched into the staff entrance at the back of the big store. The shop hadn't opened yet but a few assistants were beginning to arrive.

Dave, the security officer at the door, looked up at Strange in surprise.

'Oh, it's you again, Santa!' he said. 'I thought you were upstairs already. Did you forget something?'

'Yes, that's right,' answered Strange in as deep a voice as he could manage. 'I had to go . . . er . . . to –'

'I expect you left Rudolph on a double yellow line, didn't you, eh?' laughed Dave, who thought himself rather witty. 'Here, hold the lift for Santa! You can't expect the poor old bloke to climb all those stairs, can you? There you go, Mister Claus, fourth floor as usual. Have a nice day!'

Strange got out of the lift and walked through the toy department to Santa's Grotto. There was no one about. The winding path into the grotto was beautifully decorated with trees covered in fake snow and little toy creatures – squirrels, deer and rabbits – peeping out between the branches, but Strange wasn't interested in the décor. He was looking for his victim.

As he reached the centre of the grotto, a log cabin made to look like a gingerbread house, Strange dropped the sack with a *thump*.

*Ow!* Star put her paw over her mouth to muffle her surprised squeal. Luckily, Strange didn't hear. He pushed his hand into the sack.

*Shall I bite it?* thought Spud, but it was too late. Strange had grabbed the baseball bat. The pups heard a single, sickening *thud*, followed by a groan and the sound of a heavy body slumping on to the floor. Strange had found the real Santa, crept up behind him and clubbed him over the head!

'Now's our chance!' Spud knew they had to act fast. The two pups pushed their way out of the sack and looked around for a way out. Their eyes took a split second to adjust to the light. It was a split second too long.

'*What!*' Strange had seen them. 'You two mutts in my sack! I recognize you from the other night too – you're the ones who trampled all over my car! You little varmints!'

He raised the baseball bat again.

'*Run, Star!* Run as fast you can!' growled Spud. 'I'll try to hold him off.'

Spud turned and snarled at Strange, baring his teeth and barking ferociously. He looked fierce but he was still only a puppy; compared to Strange he was very small.

'Don't you growl at me!' said Strange and brought the baseball bat down with a *thwack*. Spud dived out of the way just in time, then he turned and growled again.

Meanwhile, Star dodged out of the grotto and into a nearby stockroom. She hid, quaking, behind a paddling pool.

'I'll get you, you little devil!' shouted Strange, a menacing sight in his jolly Santa outfit, wielding the heavy baseball bat.

*Thwack!* This time the bat grazed Spud's ear. He reckoned Star had had long enough to get away. Now it was time for him to do the same. His back paws skidding on the shiny floor, Spud decided on a surprise tactic. Instead of running away from Strange, he ran towards him, hurtling through the gap between his black, shiny boots. Strange tried to reach down to grab the pup but was hampered by his big, padded tummy. He tripped over head first and ended up doing a perfect forward roll. By the time Strange was sitting up again, Spud was gone.

'Stupid dogs,' muttered Strange, feeling rather embarrassed now. 'Getting in my way. I'm losing valuable time.'

Strange lifted the unconscious Santa under the arms and dragged him into the stockroom where Star was hiding. He tied him up with the rope and gag from the sack. Then he straightened his beard and marched out, locking the door behind him, just in time to take his place in Santa's rocking chair in the grotto. The shop's doors were open and the first customers were coming in.

## 9. Spud in the City

'Look at that puppy!' The little girl on her way to Santa's Grotto couldn't believe her eyes. 'It looks sooo real!'

*Of course I'm real!* thought Spud indignantly from his hiding place behind a large display of scooters. But then he realized, *Oh no! I'm in a toy department. She thinks I'm a toy!*

'It *is* real. It must be lost!' The girl's brother had seen Spud now. 'Come here, pup, it's OK, we won't hurt you.'

They seemed like nice children and Spud was tempted to make friends with them but the word 'lost' struck terror into his heart. *What if they take me to a dogs' home? I might never see my family again!* He started to back away and bumped into a scooter, which toppled into another scooter, which fell on to a bike. In

54

seconds there was a chaotic tangle of handlebars and wheels.

*Hmm, not a good move. I couldn't have drawn more attention to myself if I'd tried.*

Spud headed for what he thought was a funny metal staircase. He'd never seen an escalator before. He started to run down it before he realized it was moving up.

*I'll just have to run faster and . . . phew . . . faster!* puffed Spud.

Eventually, he reached the bottom. Luckily, the next escalator was going downwards. Spud realized he could simply sit on the step and be taken to the lower floor without moving a muscle.

*This is amazing! We should have one of these at home.*

By the time he'd got to the ground floor Spud was quite enjoying himself. The shop was full of exciting sights and interesting smells. It was warm and bright and there was cheerful Christmassy music playing. Better still, on the ground floor there was a huge food department.

*Mmmm, I can smell fresh bread and chocolate,* thought Spud. His tummy began to rumble. *I wonder if . . .?*

'Who let that dog in here?' The store manager had seen him. He didn't look pleased.

*Uh-oh. I don't think I'm welcome!* Spud slipped out of the open shop doors into the cold air of the busy street.

The pavement was thronging with people. Furry boots, stiletto heels, grubby trainers, shiny lace-ups – Spud had never seen so many feet so close together – and all moving so fast! He dodged his way through the forest of legs but when he reached the kerb, his path was blocked by a big red London bus, then a taxi, then another bus. The traffic was nose to tail. It was noisy and smelly too.

Then, from a side street, Spud heard the clip-clopping of horses' hooves. It was a sound he knew well from the village at home. Two handsome chestnut police horses were proudly carrying their riders side by side.

*Police officers! I could tell them about Strange and his plan*, thought Spud. *But how?* The policemen were so high off the ground they didn't even notice the small black pup looking up at them from the pavement.

The horses saw him. One of them dipped her head and snorted in a friendly way but

Spud couldn't understand. *If only I'd learned more horse language*, thought Spud despairingly as the pair passed by.

'Hello there, young'un,' growled a gentle voice behind him. Spud turned and saw a golden Labrador wearing a bright fluorescent jacket.

*Oh, thank goodness, another dog!*

'Can you help me, please?' said Spud. 'I've

got to rescue my sister who's locked in a room at the top of a shop with an unconscious man who may need medical attention, but there's a dangerous villain up there, dressed as Father Christmas, he's got the key you see, and he's going to commit a huge robbery really soon – at twelve o'clock I think – and it's my mission to stop him and –'

'Really?' the Labrador smiled indulgently. 'I think you might have been watching too many films, young fellow-me-lad. Now hop it, there's a good boy. I'm working.'

At that moment, Spud realized three things. The first was that the Labrador didn't believe a word he'd said, and Spud had to admit his garbled story did sound rather far-fetched; the second was that the Labrador was a guide dog for the blind and was too busy helping his owner to have time for a small black pup from a village far away; and the third and final thing Spud realized was that he was a very small dog in a very big city. Despite all the people around him, he was totally and completely alone.

## 10. Agent CV89

Just a few miles away across the city, the Cook family were spending the morning in London.

'All these brilliant shops!' said Mum enthusiastically after breakfast. 'I can feel some serious retail therapy coming on.'

Ben and Sophie groaned. Neither of them could understand why Mum liked shopping so much – or why it took her so long. Lara wasn't keen, either, and Dad said he'd rather eat worms than go anywhere near a big store on the Saturday before Christmas.

'That's OK,' said Mum. 'We'll split up. You can take Ben, Sophie and Lara to the London Eye and I'll take Ollie to buy his new shoes – and to look at some computer games,' she added quickly when she saw Ollie's face. 'We'll meet up at lunchtime.'

'Oh, Mum, why can't *I* go to the London Eye?' complained Ollie.

'I'm sorry, Ollie, there isn't time to do both, but you can have a special surprise treat of your own instead,' promised Mum. Ollie beamed. He liked surprises.

'Do they let dogs on the London Eye?' asked Ben.

'Not usually,' said Dad, 'but they'll make an exception for Lara. The professor's had a word with them.'

*I should think so too*, thought Lara. *I'm hardly just any old dog. Sometimes I think they forget!*

So Mum and Ollie went off to the tube station and Dad, Ben, Sophie and Lara set off for the London Eye. As they were walking along the path beside the river, looking across at the Houses of Parliament, Lara noticed a man in an old overcoat selling newspapers. He had a young dog sitting beside him with a piece of string for a lead. It was a spaniel with brown freckles on a white nose.

*I think we've met before!* thought Lara.

She wandered casually over to the dog. 'How's the mission going, Agent CV89?' she muttered, pretending to sniff a piece of paper on the ground nearby.

'Bit boring, really,' smiled the spaniel. 'We're working on a tip-off but it might not be reliable. Something to do with some secret government documents. Probably nothing to it.'

'Well, keep on your guard,' advised Lara. 'Sometimes things happen when you least expect it.'

Dad bought a newspaper from the man. 'Keep the change, mate,' he said. 'Merry Christmas!'

Ben and Sophie patted the dog, then Ben did a double take. 'Hey!' he exclaimed.

*He's recognized the spaniel too.* Lara pushed Ben hard in the back of the knees. *Be quiet, Ben! Don't say any more!*

Ben got the message, he gave Sophie a nudge and they all walked quickly on. 'Spy Dogs everywhere,' he whispered.

A few minutes later they heard a sudden commotion behind them. Lara spun round, immediately on full alert.

*Something's happened!*

A man carrying a briefcase was sprinting along the path, followed closely by the homeless newspaper seller, who had thrown off his overcoat and was running like a champion sprinter, and Agent CV89. Agent CV89 was barking fiercely and the newspaper seller was shouting, '*Stop! Police!*'

Dad and the children froze. In fact everyone on the riverbank froze, watching in shock as the spaniel caught up with the man and made a grab for the briefcase. But the man pulled out a handgun. He aimed it at the newspaper seller and stopped him in his tracks. Then he aimed it at the dog at his feet.

*Oh no! He's going to shoot!*

The spaniel remembered his training. He dived over the wall into the river and disappeared under the water.

With his gun aimed back at the newspaper seller, the man began to edge towards a landing stage, where a motorboat was moored ready for his getaway.

Lara's mind raced through her options. *He's got his back to us, so he won't see me if I make a dash for him,* she thought. *But he's too far away. By the time I get there it will be too late. If only there was something I could throw, like a rope or —* Then she remembered. *The professor's secret weapon! I haven't got a gun to fire it but maybe I could throw it?*

Lara grabbed Sophie's rucksack from her back and tore it open. She pulled out the plastic bag with the bright blue ball inside and ripped that open too. The man was at the end of the landing stage, about to get into the boat. *He's too far away. I can't throw it that distance.*

Then Lara remembered the slings she had seen people use for throwing balls to dogs in the park at home. She grabbed the end of Ben's woolly scarf, pulled it sharply off him and quickly folded it in half to make a simple sling. She put the ball into the sling and, holding the ends of the scarf between her teeth, twirled the whole thing round and round above her head before hurling the bright blue ball through the air towards her target. *Yes! A perfect hit.* Just as the man was about to start the engine, the bullet hit his back and exploded, covering him with fine blue dust.

No one watching could believe the result. The man instantly began to laugh and laugh. Tears rolled down his cheeks as he chuckled. He laughed so much that he couldn't stand. You'd think he had heard the funniest joke in the world. 'Hee hee hee!' he went. 'Oh, ha ha! Hee hee hee!' He couldn't hold the briefcase, or the gun. He dropped them both and collapsed on his back in the boat, holding his tummy and waving his legs in the air, laughing and laughing and laughing.

Agent CV89 was a good swimmer. He reappeared in the water beside the boat and retrieved the briefcase in a very professional way.

The newspaper seller took possession of the gun and, together with some other unlikely-looking officers — a road sweeper and a traffic warden — he frogmarched the robber away — with some difficulty, as he was still bent double with laughter.

The family looked at Lara in amazement. Sophie gave her a hug. 'You are FANTASTIC, Lara!' she said.

*Just helping out a colleague!* smiled Lara. *The lad did well for his first mission. Well, what are we waiting for? Let's go and see what this London Eye is all about!*

## 11. The Pickpocket

*I can't just sit here feeling sorry for myself.* Spud had decided to give himself a pep talk. *I need to get reinforcements.*

Spud knew that Lara and the rest of the family were in London somewhere; all he had to do was work out how to find them.

He dodged out of the way as a young man, talking loudly on his mobile phone, almost tripped over him. *That's it! Ben always has his phone with him!*

Spud looked around. There was a public phonebox further down the street but he probably couldn't even open the door, let alone reach up to the keypad. *Maybe I could borrow someone's phone. It is an emergency, after all.*

He walked slowly along, looking up at the people. They probably all had phones but they all seemed to be safely tucked away. As he passed the door of a jeweller's shop, he noticed a man and a woman just inside, looking at a gold bracelet.

'Darling Pumpkin,' cooed the woman. 'It's beautiful! But it's far too expensive!'

'Nothing's too much for my little Cupcake,' said the man. 'And it *is* Cupcake and Pumpkin's

first Christmas, isn't it? Go on, sweetie – try it on!'

*Oh yuck!* thought Spud in horror. *How soppy!* Then he thought again. As Cupcake tried on the bracelet, she put her expensive handbag down on the floor, and there, sticking out of it, was a small gold-coloured mobile phone.

*Here goes!* Spud dashed into the shop. Just as he reached the phone, it started to ring. Cupcake bent to pick it up and saw Spud standing guiltily beside her bag.

'Oh, Pumpkin, look, a sweet little puppy-wuppy!' she gushed as ten pink polished nails reached down to lift Spud up.

*Oh no, you don't!* Spud ran out of the shop as fast as he could go. *That was close!*

Inside the stockroom on the fourth floor, Star too had been doing her best to continue their mission. The first thing she did after Strange had left the room was run to check on the unconscious Santa. It took her a while but she managed to chew through the ropes around his wrists and then carefully do the same with his gag. After that she gradually pushed and pulled until she managed to get him into the recovery position.

*I'm glad Mum gave us those first-aid lessons*, she thought as she turned the old man over on his side on the floor and made sure his airways were clear.

She tried barking for help but soon realized

that no one could hear her. The shop was busy now and Christmas music was playing loudly on every floor.

Star had a good look round to see if there was another way out, but the stockroom had no windows and only one door and the lock was one she had no chance of picking.

All she could do was keep an eye on the casualty and wait. *But it's OK*, thought Star, *because my brother's out there and he won't let me down!*

Spud's narrow escape in the jeweller's had given him an idea. *I have to think like a thief*, he said to himself. *I've got no choice.* He remembered the force that Strange had used to hit the back of poor old Santa's head, and shivered. *It could even be a matter of life or death.*

He trotted along the street until he came to a cafe. Two teenage girls — one dark and one fair — were drinking smoothies and chatting. The one with dark hair had put her handbag safely under the table. At least she thought it was safe. She didn't notice a small black pup slithering on his tummy towards her. Being very careful not to touch their feet, Spud pushed his nose into the bag, searching for a phone. *Yes!* He picked it up gently in his mouth and pulled it slowly out of the bag. *If this one rings, I've had it!* But the phone didn't ring. Like an experienced pickpocket, Spud was out of the cafe in seconds. No one had noticed. *If they see that on closed-circuit TV later, they'll get a shock!* chuckled Spud.

He ducked into an alleyway and found an old cocktail stick lying on the ground by some dustbins. *Exactly what I need! Pups' paws aren't designed for mobile phones.*

Holding the stick in his mouth, Spud tapped out Ben's number and waited. It was ringing.

*Please, answer, Ben! Don't let it go to voicemail!*

## 12. On the London Eye

The clear oval pod was climbing slowly round the big wheel of the London Eye and Dad was just pointing out a funny-looking building nicknamed 'The Gherkin' when Ben heard his ringtone.

'I wonder who this is? I don't recognize the number.' Ben pulled the phone out of his pocket. 'Hello?'

Instead of an answering voice there was a torrent of urgent barking – it sounded like one of the pups, although Ben couldn't be sure. Lara was sure, though. She recognized Spud's voice straight away and jumped up to put her head beside the phone.

'Oh, I see, it's for you, Lara!' laughed Ben. Then he realized from Lara's face that something was wrong.

'You're *where*?' barked Lara. 'What about Star? *What?!* Stanley Strange! When? Midday? But it's almost that now! OK, go back to the shop and wait. I'll be there as soon as I can.'

'What's the matter, Lara?' asked Sophie. By now their pod was creeping over the top of the wheel. The sun was out and the views were fantastic, but no one noticed. They were all looking at Lara.

Lara grabbed Dad's tourist map of London and pointed to the store. Then she pointed at Ben's phone and barked urgently.

'Spud and Star are in that shop?' asked Ben. 'But how? Why?'

*I haven't got time for this*, thought Lara

desperately. *I've got to get there. I've got to stop Strange and rescue Star!*

She looked down at the city spread out so far below them. The slow ride up had been such fun, but now she felt like a prisoner trapped high in the air.

*It's going to take ages to reach the ground. I might as well try and explain*, she thought.

Lara took Ben's phone and, using Dad's pen between her teeth, carefully spelled out two words as if she was going to send a text.

**strange santa**

'Strange Santa? Do you mean there's a strange Santa in the shop?' asked Sophie.

Lara nodded vigorously and then pointed meaningfully at the word 'Strange' and began to mime playing the mouth organ. For a minute everyone looked blank.

'I've got it!' said Ben. ' When we were carol singing – that horrible man at End House – his name was Stanley Strange, wasn't it? Is he the strange Santa, Lara? Is that why Spud and Star are there?'

*Yes! Well done, Ben – and Star is in danger too.*

*Oh, why doesn't this big wheel thing move any faster?!*

Lara looked as anxious as she could and pointed at the number twelve on Dad's watch. Now Ben and Sophie understood perfectly, although Dad was still looking baffled.

'Something bad is going to happen in the shop at twelve o'clock, Dad,' explained Sophie.

'Yes, something that involves Stanley Strange – that man who nearly ran us all over. I think he might be disguised as Santa Claus,' added Ben.

*That's right! That's right!* barked Lara, nodding.

'*WHAT?!*' said Dad, suddenly looking horrified. 'But that's where Mum's taking Ollie for his special treat – to see Santa in that shop. We've got to get there – and fast!'

### 13. Strange Santa

Spud turned off the phone with a sigh of relief. This mission had got a bit too big for him and he was glad to feel that Lara had taken charge. *I've got my orders now, I must go back to the shop and wait*, he thought. *Oh, but first I must return this phone.*

He trotted round the corner just in time to see the two girls setting off up the road, their bags firmly over their shoulders. *Oh no, I'm too late! What am I going to do?*

There was nothing for it. Holding the phone carefully in his mouth, Spud ran up to the dark-haired girl and sat down on the pavement right in front of her, blocking her path. Then he put the phone down carefully by her feet and looked her directly in the eye. He cocked his head in what he hoped was his cute puppy look. *Yours, I think?*

'My phone! Oh, I must have dropped it!' said the girl. 'What a clever dog! Thank you! Thank you! That's amazing!'

Spud felt embarrassed. *She doesn't know that I took it in the first place. There's no way I should be thanked for giving it back.* He hung his head as the girl patted him gratefully, then gave her hand a quick lick and scurried off into the crowd.

As Spud made his way back down the street, the big department store loomed in front of him. He gazed up to the fourth floor. *I wonder what's happening in there?* He thought. *And, more to the point, what's going to happen at twelve o'clock?*

Up in the toy department, Mum and Ollie were standing in the queue for Santa's Grotto. Mum was weighed down with carrier bags and Ollie was proudly carrying his new shoes, still in their box. When Mum told Ollie what his special treat would be, he was thrilled. 'I've never been to see Father Christmas in a shop before!' he said.

Even now, in the queue, he couldn't stand still and kept hopping from foot to foot, peering at all the Christmassy scenery and exclaiming as he spotted different little animals hidden in the branches. 'I wonder what Santa will say to me? Will I get a present? Hey, look, Mum, a squirrel! Look, it's moving! It's holding a nut in its paws! What kind of present will I get, Mum? Oh, wow! Look, there's a sort of house in there! Is that where Santa is? Are we going in soon?'

There were some nice young women dressed as Santa's elves directing the queue and Ollie noticed that one of them came out of the gingerbread house looking a bit concerned and whispered something to another, but he was too excited to let it bother him.

Inside the grotto, Stanley Strange was doing a terrible job of impersonating Santa. Strange was a clever man who could have turned his brains to very good use if he'd chosen to. In front of a computer – any computer – he was truly a wizard, but doing something as simple as talking to a small child was quite beyond him.

'What do you want for Christmas?' he snarled at a four-year-old. The little boy was shy and kept his thumb firmly in his mouth.

'Come on, come on, I haven't got all day,' said Strange. 'And if you keep sucking your thumb like that all you'll get is braces on your teeth. Here, take this.' He passed the child a present from the real Santa's sack. 'Merry Christmas. Ho ho! Next, please!'

The only time Strange brightened up was when one little girl said she'd like the latest computerized toy robot for Christmas. 'Ah, well, that's an interesting choice,' he said and started a long explanation of exactly how it worked and all the different ways that it could

have been improved. 'I think the manufacturers were cutting corners,' he confided. 'Any fool can see that an infrared detector would have improved its efficiency, and personally I would have added a sensor control feature as well.'

The little girl was only five and couldn't understand a word. Strange didn't notice at first and continued to bombard her with facts until the little girl began to cry.

'What! You mean you don't know the difference between a megabyte and a megapixel,' said Strange impatiently. 'For heaven's sake! The toy would be wasted on you. Stick to dollies and teddies, little girl. Merry Christmas. Ho ho! Stop blubbing. Next!'

'What on earth's happened to Santa?' said one of the elves to another. 'He's usually so good with the kids.'

'I know!' agreed the other elf. 'You'd hardly believe it was the same man!'

'And another thing,' added her friend. 'Why does he keep looking at his watch?'

The secret Santa checked his watch one more time. The seconds were ticking. When the big hand and little hand met at twelve, he would be a multi-millionaire.

## 14. Follow That Dog!

The moment the doors of their pod slid open, Dad, Ben, Sophie and Lara leapt out and began to sprint towards the road. They had to reach that department store. There wasn't a minute to lose.

'We'll get a taxi,' said Dad, frantically waving both arms about in a windmill motion as he saw a black London cab driving towards them. The cab sailed by. There was already a passenger sitting in the back, reading a newspaper.

*You have to look for one that has its light on*, thought Lara. *Dad's in such a panic he's not thinking straight*.

She spotted a cab with the word 'TAXI' lit up on its roof and calmly raised a paw to catch the driver's eye. The cab pulled to a halt, the driver astonished to be hailed by a black-and-white dog.

'I've seen it all now,' he said.

The family bundled into the back and they set off across the river. But the journey was painfully slow. It seemed like everyone in the world was out in London that morning. Cars, buses, motorbikes and taxis jammed the roads while groups of shoppers threaded their way through them. Every traffic light seemed to be stuck on red as gangs of people poured over the crossings, laughing and chatting.

Lara pointed at Dad's watch. *It's almost quarter to twelve! We're never going to get there at this rate.* Then she pawed at the taxi door.

Ben took the hint. 'Lara thinks we'll be quicker on foot,' he said.

'Yes, I think you're right, Lara,' said Dad. He paid the driver and the family tumbled out and began trying to push their way through the crowded streets.

'Which way, Dad? Up here?' asked Sophie. The children had never been to this part of London before and had no idea where they were or where they were going.

Dad wasn't really sure, either. 'It's a long time since I was last here,' he said, putting on his

glasses to look at the map. 'I think we take the
next turning on the right – or is it the left? Oh,
sorry, I do beg your pardon!' Ben and Sophie
tried not to laugh. A man beside them was
carrying a large Christmas tree over his shoulder
and Dad had just apologized to the tree.

Lara's training meant she could memorize a
route in seconds. She took one long look at the
map and began to run ahead, leading the family
down a series of tiny side streets and alleys,
away from the crowds. *No time to lose. My pups*

*are in peril*. Lara was sprinting now and the others all ran as fast as they could to keep up with her, but soon Sophie started to get a stitch and Dad was puffing hard.

Lara was just as fit as she always had been; football practice with Ben and judo lessons with Sophie (Sophie was coming on well) kept her in tip-top condition. *If I go on ahead I might get there in time, but I'd have to leave the others behind*. She quickly assessed the situation. *The children will be OK with their dad — even if he is beginning to go rather red in the face*. With a wave of her paw, Lara began to run flat out like a greyhound. *See you later, guys!* The family were soon left far behind.

Lara couldn't avoid the busy roads for long. Suddenly, the narrow alleyway became a broader road and before she knew it, she was out in the traffic again. The cars and buses were at a standstill and the pavement was jammed too. There were shoppers everywhere! A group of tourists were marvelling at the Christmas lights, all gazing upwards and taking photographs. Lara dived through their legs, only to come straight up against a double buggy carrying identical twins, both bawling loudly. *This is hopeless!*

Then Lara noticed one vehicle that managed to keep moving. It was a racing bike ridden by a messenger in Lycra shorts and a state-of-the-art helmet. He had a carrier box on the back of his bike and was darting expertly through the traffic at top speed. *Now's my chance!* thought Lara as he drew near. With one great bound she leapt towards the moving bike and landed on top of the box. The messenger felt the weight increase and glanced sharply to his

right; Lara leant quickly sideways in the opposite direction, ducking out of his line of vision. He glanced to his left and Lara ducked to the right. He too was in a hurry. He hadn't time to stop and investigate. He put his head down and pedalled swiftly on with Lara riding triumphantly behind. *What a perfect way to hitch a lift!*

## 15. Fire!

Mum and Ollie had reached the head of the queue. Ollie was bursting with excitement – at last he was going to meet Santa Claus! They went into the gingerbread house and through a little wooden door into a room filled with shiny Christmas decorations. There was an enormous Christmas tree and a very good imitation of a crackling log fire. Santa was sitting on a large, wooden rocking chair in the middle of the room with his sack of presents beside him. He was dressed as Ollie expected in a bright red outfit trimmed with white fur, a black belt and big black boots. He had a fat tummy and a long curly white beard and moustache. Yet something wasn't quite right. Above the whiskers, Santa's eyes looked anything but merry and twinkling; instead they darted from side to side, looking shifty and tense.

The elf took Ollie's hand and led him to Santa's side, then she moved away. Ollie stared up at those pale blue eyes. He had the oddest feeling that he'd seen them somewhere before.

'Right,' said Santa in an off-hand way. 'What's your name and what do you want for Christmas?'

Ollie hesitated. This wasn't what he'd expected at all. He looked hard into Santa's face. 'My name's Ollie,' he said at last. 'What's yours?'

Strange gave a guilty start, then he turned on Ollie angrily. 'What kind of a question is that?' he snapped, in a voice quite different from the one he'd used before. 'I'm Santa Claus *obviously*, you stupid boy. Here, take your present and get out of here before I lose my temper. Go on – scram!'

'I knew it!' said Ollie. 'I've heard you say that before! You're not Santa at all. You're that horrible man from the village – the one who hates children!'

Strange leapt to his feet, his face white with anger. He couldn't believe he'd been recognized!

It was a disaster. His whole plan hinged on the fact that he was wearing the perfect disguise. That way no one would ever know who he was.

'You little liar!' he said in a menacing voice that sent shudders down Ollie's spine. 'I don't know what you're talking about. I've never seen you before in my life!

But in his rage Strange had knocked his false beard sideways – his whole face could suddenly be seen.

'Get security quickly,' called out one of the elf helpers. 'That man isn't our Santa at all. He's an imposter!'

Strange knew the game was up. Even if he managed to steal the money now, the police would know who he was.

But the thought of all that cash was just too much for him. He decided to go ahead with his plan and take his chance. *I'll be out of the country in hours*, he thought. *They'll never track me down.*

Pushing Ollie roughly out of his way, Strange ran from the grotto, past the startled queues of waiting children and parents. 'Go home, the lot of you! Christmas is cancelled!' he yelled. Everyone watched in astonishment as Strange sprinted to the top of the escalator. He looked around, his evil mind weighing up the options. He was on the top floor of the store. The imposter Santa peered down over the balcony to all the floors below. He saw a security guard talking into his walkie-talkie. Another guard saw Strange and pointed. Two more were making their way to the escalator – they were closing in. Strange needed to act fast. He pulled out the big box of matches that Star and Spud had seen in his sack, struck one and put it back into the box. The flame from the match set light to all the other matches inside and soon the whole box was on fire.

'Oh, whoops!' laughed Strange as he hurled the box over the balcony into a huge display of Christmas crackers on the ground floor. 'I seem to have started a . . . FIRE!'

Within seconds the whole display was alight. The air was filled with the sound of hundreds of tiny explosions as all the crackers exploded, one by one, hurling little plastic toys – whistles, compasses and rubber dinosaurs – out into the shop.

Straight away the fire alarms began to ring. A few people screamed; others urged them to keep calm. Everyone began hurrying towards the exits, anxious to get as far away from the flames as possible. The security guards forgot about Strange and started to help children and the elderly out of the building instead.

Up on the top floor, Mum and Ollie joined the crowds making for the stairs. 'It's all right, Mum,' said Ollie. 'I know what to do. The firemen who came to our school said if there's a fire, you've got to "Get out, stay out and call the fire brigade out!"'

'That's absolutely right, Ollie,' said Mum, holding his hand tightly. 'And luckily, the smoke hasn't reached this part of the building yet. We've just got to get downstairs as fast as we can.'

The noise of the fire alarm reached every corner of the store. In the stockroom it was loud enough to make the real Santa stir.

*Thank goodness, he's coming round*, thought Star. She licked his face and hands and yapped in his ear, hoping to bring him back to consciousness. Soon the old man was sitting up, rubbing the lump on the back of his head and feeling very confused.

'Where am I? What happened?' he muttered. 'The last thing I remember, I was just about to start my day's work . . .' He looked down at the torn ropes and gag lying beside him on the floor. 'What's all this? And where did you come from, doggie?' he said. 'And *what on earth* is that terrible noise?'

Star had never heard a fire alarm before. At first all she knew was that it hurt her sensitive doggie ears, but then she started to smell the smoke. *We've got to get out of here*, she thought, jumping and scratching helplessly at the locked door.

The department store was in chaos. Crowds thronged towards the exits. The security guards and staff members were trying to stay calm. People came rushing out of changing rooms in their underwear and from the shoe department in their socks. Everyone had the same idea. They just wanted to get out.

But one person had no intention of leaving the building. Stanley Strange was pleased with his handiwork. Once the fire had started, he'd taken advantage of the confusion and made a dash into one of the offices on the fourth floor.

'Ha! Just as I'd planned!' he laughed. 'Things are starting to go my way again.'

The woman who worked in the office had left her desk in a hurry. She hadn't stopped to turn off her computer. It was still switched on, and still linked to the shop's main network.

Strange's eyes lit up and he grinned his first genuine smile of the day. 'I can get to work straight away!' He sat down on the swivel chair and began to tap on the keyboard, first slowly and then much faster. An eerie calm came over him as he stared unblinkingly at the lit screen.

He didn't hear the sound of the fire alarm or the clatter of people evacuating the building. He didn't hear the barking puppy in the stockroom or the real Santa shouting for help. Strange was far, far away, in a happy, peaceful place, wrapped in his own little cyberworld. In ten minutes, he would be a multi-millionaire.

## 16. Lara to the Rescue!

Lara arrived at the entrance to the store just as the fire alarm began to ring. Spud was waiting at the doorway. He had never been so glad to see her.

'What's that terrible noise, Mum?' he asked, covering his ears with his paws. Before Lara could answer, they heard someone shouting inside the shop. 'There's a fire on the ground floor! Everybody leave the building!'

Spud leapt away from the door. 'That's got to be something to do with Stanley Strange,' he barked. 'I bet that's why he had the box of matches.'

'I think Mum and Ollie are inside!' gasped Lara, 'And Star – did you say she was locked in a stockroom?'

'Yes, she's with the real Santa,' replied Spud, 'on the fourth floor, near the grotto.'

By now there was a steady stream of people leaving the shop; soon it would be a torrent and then a flood. Lara tried hard to contain the rush of anxiety that was racing through her body. *Keep calm; remember your training.*

She pointed to a spot across the road, in sight of the shop but a safe distance away. 'Wait over there and look out for Dad, Ben and Sophie. They'll be here soon. I'm going in.'

'But Mum . . .' said Spud. He too remembered what the firemen had told Ollie's class at school. 'Get out, stay out, call the fire brigade out.'

'I'm a Spy Dog, Spud. I'm trained for emergencies. You take care of the family and let me take care of secret Santa.'

'But Mum,' whined Spud. 'It's dangerous.'

Lara looked her puppy in the eye. 'Sometimes a Spy Dog has no choice,' she woofed. 'Try not to worry.' Spud watched as his mum bounded into the store.

It was chaos! Hundreds of people were hurrying down the shop's staircases as Lara fought her way up. Some of them tried to push her downwards with them. One man actually grabbed her collar and forcibly dragged her down several stairs.

*Sorry, I know you're trying to help*, thought Lara as she bared her teeth in a snarl that made him let go of her collar instantly. The noise of the fire alarm was hurting her ears. People were screaming, children crying and all the lights had gone off.

As Lara reached the second floor, she heard a familiar voice.

'Lara! Have you come to rescue us?'

*It's Ollie – and there's Mum too, thank goodness!*

Ollie threw his arms round Lara's neck and gave her a hug, 'It's OK, Lara, we'll be out in a minute and then the fire brigade will come.'

*No, Ollie, it's not OK. Star is trapped in a locked room. I've got to rescue her.*

Lara pulled herself away, gave Ollie a quick lick and pushed on upwards past a very large man in a ski jacket.

Ollie couldn't understand what she was doing. 'Lara!' he bellowed, turning back to try and get a glimpse of her as she disappeared into the crowd. 'Lara, come back!'

Mum couldn't understand it, either. 'We can't stop, Ollie. Lara must have her reasons. We've got to keep going!' Ollie's eyes filled with tears but he knew his mum was right. They hurried down the last flights of stairs and out into the cold fresh air.

By the time Lara reached the third floor, the last few people were hurrying downwards. Soon the staircase was deserted. With her heart thumping and her mouth dry, Lara carried bravely on up to the fourth floor alone.

The toy department was deserted. An empty buggy stood in the middle of the floor and some abandoned shopping bags lay on their sides beside the till. It was clear that everyone had left in a hurry. Lara looked round quickly. *Where's Santa's Grotto?*

She raced over to that corner of the department and into the warren of offices and stockrooms behind. The fire alarm was still making a terrible noise but she thought she could hear the faint sound of barking and shouting through the clamour. As Lara passed an open office door, she stopped suddenly. Someone in a red coat was sitting with his back to her, in front of a computer.

*It's Santa! But is it the real one or Stanley Strange in disguise?*

The man was muttering quietly to himself. 'OK, I've disabled the sprinkler system so the fire can really get going. No chance of the fire brigade getting up here for a good while yet . . . Now on to the next part of my plan.'

*It's Strange. He must be mad! Doesn't he want to be rescued?* thought Lara, but there was no time to worry about that now. She had to find the others. It wasn't hard. The real Santa was beating his fists on the stockroom door and shouting, 'Help! Help! Get me out of here!' at the top of his voice. Star was barking along with him and scratching at the door. Lara had to bark her loudest to make herself heard.

'It's Mum, Star. Don't worry, I'm here and I'm going to get you out!'

She quickly examined the lock. *Oh no, it's high security. I can't pick it. It needs a special swipe card. If only I had more time . . .*

But Lara knew she had hardly any time at all. *I'll have to break the door down.*

She ran back to the office where Strange was still bent over the computer, deep in concentration. There was a small metal filing cabinet on wheels just by the door.

*This will do!* Lara began to push it out into the corridor. *Don't look round, please don't look round!* She didn't need to worry. Strange was still far away in his own little world, muttering about passwords and bank account numbers.

'Stand away from the door, Star. Get Santa away too,' barked Lara. 'Be quick! Tell me when you're ready.'

Now it was Star's turn to think fast. *How can*

*I get him away from the door? He doesn't understand me and he's desperate to get out!*

As Santa stood hammering on the door, Star picked up one of Strange's ropes in her mouth and looped it quickly round his ankles. Then she gave a short, sharp tug so that the old man overbalanced and fell sideways to the floor.

'What on earth?' he exclaimed. 'I thought you were helping!'

'Ready!' barked Star to Lara. 'But be quick!'

Lara had lined the filing cabinet up with the door some distance away down the corridor. She started to push it along, running behind, then ran faster and faster and, as it gathered speed and momentum, finally sent it flying straight into the door.

*Crash!*

It worked! The force of the heavy metal cabinet had burst open the lock. The door flew open, narrowly missing Santa and Star, and the cabinet rolled in, closely followed by Lara.

'Goodness gracious me!' said Santa. 'We've been rescued, my little puppy friend, by a dog who looks just like you!'

Lara led the way to the emergency exit. Santa

jogged after her, carrying Star. By now most of the floor below was filled with smoke and flames, and smoke was beginning to billow up to the fourth floor too, but the emergency stairway was still clear. It was getting hot and Santa was sweating.

*Go straight down*, barked Lara. *If it gets smoky crawl on the floor — there will be more air there. You should be OK — but hurry!*

Santa didn't need to be told. He was surprisingly nimble for an old man and disappeared down the stairs at top speed, holding Star tightly in his arms.

Lara was left standing alone at the top of the stairs as the whole building began to fill with fire.

## 17. The Great Escape

It was decision time for Lara. She knew that the fire would soon engulf the shop, and a very big part of her longed to follow Santa and Star down the stairs to safety.

*Stanley Strange is a baddie*, she thought. *But should I risk everything to capture him? Even the professor would understand if I failed to make an arrest in this life-threatening situation.*

Yet still Lara hesitated. She knew there was something even more important to consider. *Baddie or not, Strange is in danger too. I can't save myself and not him. Somehow I've got to get us both out of this building — and alive!*

Lara bounded back towards the office where she'd last seen Strange.

The toy department was filling with smoke, so she slammed the fire safety door, hoping to buy a few minutes from the flames. *Phew! Luckily, the offices and stockrooms are still clear.* She hurtled into the office and skidded to a halt. *He's disappeared!*

Lara looked around wildly and then began a quick but thorough search of all the other rooms. *Nothing!* At the end of the corridor she noticed a small flight of concrete stairs. A door at the top of the stairs was partly open and Lara could see blue sky and feel a rush of cold air. *Those stairs lead to the roof.* It was then that Lara heard an almost deafening engine noise – a helicopter was hovering just above the building.

*Oh no! So that's why he didn't mind about the fire,* thought Lara. *He's got an accomplice to airlift him from the roof!*

Now Lara was filled with rage. Strange didn't care about the poor old man he left unconscious in that locked room. He didn't care about all the people working and shopping in the store. He didn't care about the fire officers risking their lives to put out the blaze. No. He knew he'd be nice and safe in his helicopter and all he cared about was the stolen money in his bank account!

Lara had done a lot of running that day but

this time she ran faster than ever before. The helicopter was hovering over the building with a rope ladder dangling from its door. As Lara reached the roof, she saw Strange, still dressed as Father Christmas, climbing on to the first rung of the ladder.

She threw herself towards him, barking and growling. *If only I can reach him in time. I'll grab his leg and pull him down!*

The helicopter pilot had seen her and began to lift up and away from the roof with Strange still climbing the ladder. He was almost out of reach. *Maybe I can still get him.* It was a risky move but Lara decided to give it a go. Imposter Santa was dangling dangerously on the ladder. He swooped by and Lara leapt. She grabbed a boot and hung on. She felt Strange kicking at her nose but her teeth gripped tighter. *I've got you, you evil man.*

'Oh no you don't, poochie,' laughed Santa Strange. The helicopter rose higher and she winced as Strange kicked off his black boot and Lara fell to the roof with a *thud*. She lay on her side, winded, the boot still firmly in her jaws. The helicopter was rising quickly now. Lara righted herself and watched as one-booted

Santa climbed up the ladder and into the helicopter. She growled angrily as Strange blew her a kiss. *I hate it when baddies get away!*

Strange was relieved. Things hadn't gone entirely according to plan but he was still a multi-millionaire. The store's Christmas takings had been successfully transferred to his account. He looked out at the furious barking dog on the roof. He supposed she must be a police dog, although he'd never seen quite such a funny-looking one before. Well, she was too late now and she wouldn't be able to get downstairs in a hurry. The fire would have reached the stairways by this time. The dog was doomed.

He blew another kiss and gave her his best sarcastic, Santa-type wave. 'Merry Christmas, doggie!' he shouted. 'Ho ho ho!'

## 18. Now or Never

On the pavement far below, the Cook family and the pups were staring anxiously upwards. Spud had spotted Mum and Ollie as soon as they came hurrying out of the store and they'd all met up with Dad and the older children when they'd arrived soon afterwards.

The shop had been safely evacuated in minutes, and fire engines, police cars and ambulances had all arrived in a clamour of sirens. The police kept the crowds at a safe distance while the fire officers set about their work.

A cheer went up when the real Santa emerged, carrying Star. They were the last to leave the building. Mr Cook dashed forward to claim the pup and Santa was delighted to be able to reunite her with her family.

'But what about Lara?' said Ben. 'And Stanley Strange? Where are they? Why haven't they come out?'

Star could only look sadly back at him. *I don't know, Ben. I don't know where they are.*

Then the helicopter appeared and the crowd gasped as they saw the scarlet-and-white figure of Stanley Strange climbing the rope ladder and making his getaway. A parapet round the edge of the roof meant they couldn't see a black-and-white dog leaping desperately upwards as the helicopter flew away.

Spud and Star couldn't stand it any longer. They ran towards the building but were caught by a burly fireman. 'Sorry, little guys,' he said. 'Far too dangerous for doggies.'

The central part of the building was engulfed in flames and the fire was spreading higher all the time. The fire brigade were working tirelessly trying to contain it.

The fireman returned the wriggling puppies to Mr and Mrs Cook. 'Our other dog is in there,' said Dad, the panic rising in his voice.

'I'm sorry, sir,' said the fireman. 'I'm afraid it doesn't look too good.' Sophie and Ben looked at each other in horror. Sophie's eyes

filled with tears. 'If she's up at the top of the building, I don't think we'll be able to save her.'

Lara *was* at the top of the building and she knew she had to save herself. *Keep calm, Lara, keep calm*, she muttered. *You're trained for tricky situations and this is just another one.* Lara thought back to some of the scrapes she'd been in. *I've been shot at and I've dangled on a rope down a mountain crevasse. I've been in lots of high-speed chases and I've ridden on the roof of a train . . . that was pretty hairy.*

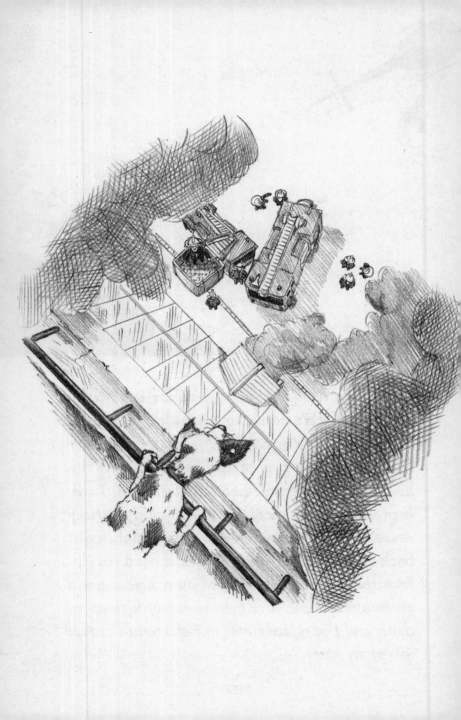

She looked at the smoke belching out of the doorway behind her. *But this is probably as bad as it gets!*

She looked down towards the street at the mass of fire engines and flashing blue lights. *Way too far to jump but could I climb down somehow?*

She peered over the edge of the parapet. *No, I would just be climbing into the fire.*

She ran over the rooftop looking all around. The buildings opposite were far away across the street but there was a block of flats next door that was much nearer. *The roof is a little lower than this one. Maybe, somehow, I could jump across?*

*Who am I kidding?* thought Lara. *I'm good at the long jump but not that good. I'd just fall straight down through the gap. Unless . . . unless . . .*

Then Lara had an idea. She held her breath and raced back down the stairs and into the stockroom. She thought she'd seen some large outdoor toys in there and, sure enough, there was the paddling pool that Star had hidden behind, a Wendy house, a couple of slides and, *Yes!,* a small but very bouncy trampoline.

*Hurry! Hurry!* muttered Lara through gritted teeth as she dragged the trampoline through the corridor. Her oxygen was running out so she was forced to take in a deep breath. Lara let go of the trampoline as she coughed and choked, the black smoke filling her lungs. *Don't give up*, she thought. *Spud and Star need their mum*. Eyes watering and lungs aching, Lara hauled the trampoline slowly and painfully up each of the steps and out on to the roof.

*Crash!*

The ceiling inside had collapsed. The corridor behind her was completely blocked with rubble and smoke. Now there really was no going back.

Her teeth aching, Lara dragged the trampoline to the edge of the roof, just across from the block of flats. *No more choices*, she thought. *I've got to make this work!*

Lara climbed on to the trampoline and began to test its bounce, pushing her back legs hard towards the springs and raising her paws in the air. *I'll need to get as much of a spring as I can from this – I'm bouncing for my life!*

Down on the pavement, Sophie caught a glimpse of her beloved pet suddenly appearing in the air above the parapet and immediately disappearing again.

'Look! It's Lara!' she shouted, pointing.

'What on earth is she doing?' said Dad as Lara appeared again. 'This is no time to be having fun!'

'She's trying to escape, Dad!' said Ben. 'Look, she's aiming for the roof of the building next door.'

Lara got off the trampoline and walked back to the other side of the roof. She stopped, took a deep breath and stared hard ahead. *If I stay here, I'm going to be a barbecued dog*, she thought. *Jumping to the next building is a huge risk, but there's a small chance I can make it.*

The whole crowd hushed as they all gazed upwards, willing her on. Then Ollie's voice could be heard shouting into the silence. 'Go on, Lara, you can do it!'

Straight away, Spud and Star joined in with a torrent of encouraging barks and soon, everyone else was shouting too, their voices rising up and giving Lara support just when she needed it.

*Yes, I can! I can do it!* thought Lara determinedly as she started to sprint towards the trampoline. *It's now or never!*

Lara sprinted like an Olympian. Using the

trampoline as
a springboard,
she threw
herself
forward,
across the edge
of the building and over the yawning chasm towards the next-door roof. It seemed to take forever. She felt herself flying through the cold air. She even had time to look down at the small faces below. Then she felt herself dropping down and down.

*Yikes, I'm not going to make it!* Lara's paws did the breaststroke in mid-air as she tried to gain a few extra centimetres.

The crowd gasped as the dog flew across the gap between the buildings. Ollie shut his eyes tightly. Sophie's mouth was wide open. Ben had his fists clenched. 'Go Lara. Go girl!' he urged.

Lara saw the roof rise to meet her. The Spy Dog felt a sharp pain as she hit the concrete with massive force, almost knocking herself out. She had landed on the very edge of the roof. She rolled over once, twice, then lay still, catching her breath.

*Am I alive?* She knew she had some broken ribs. *But I can wiggle my legs.* At last she stood up and waved a shaky paw at the people below.

A huge cheer came up from the crowd. Spud and Star leapt in the air as if they too were on trampolines. Mum burst into tears and hugged Dad, Santa, then several complete strangers.

Ben and Sophie did a high-five. Lara was safe!

'Amazing!' cheered one of the onlookers.

'She's a Super Dog . . .' yelled someone else from the crowd.

'No,' corrected Ollie, doing a little victory dance. 'She's a Spy Dog.'

## 19. And a Happy New Year!

All the Cook family, including Lara and the pups, were sitting round the table having Christmas dinner. This year they were joined by a guest who was becoming more and more like another member of the family – Professor Cortex.

'More turkey, Professor?' asked Dad. His purple paper hat was at a jaunty angle on the back of his head and he was brandishing a carving knife.

'I won't say no!' laughed the scientist, in a bright pink paper crown, passing his plate.

'What about you two pups?' smiled Dad. 'I bet you could manage another little sausage? Or a bacon roll? Or maybe both?'

Spud and Star couldn't stop their tails from wagging today. Thick snow had fallen

overnight and when they woke up, the whole village looked like a Christmas card. They'd both found their stockings brimming with presents and now there was all this delicious food. This just had to be the best day ever!

Lara looked proudly at her two pups, washed and brushed in their best collars and using their knives and forks politely. They had been so pleased to have her back safe and sound that they hadn't thought to ask what had happened to Stanley Strange, but the professor had told Lara all about it. Now he was telling everyone else.

'So, his accomplice landed the helicopter in a car park in the middle of nowhere,' continued the professor. 'Ooh yes, please. I can never resist roast potatoes! These ones are lovely and crispy too. Mmm. Now where was I?'

'In the middle of nowhere,' prompted Sophie.

'Oh yes, well, then they transferred to a stolen car. In fact they switched cars twice more and then drove to a disused airport where a private jet was waiting to take them to Cuba.'

'Wow!' said Ben. 'That must have taken some planning.'

'Yes, and they were pretty confident they wouldn't be caught. In fact, if it hadn't been for these two fine young pups, I'd say they would definitely have got away.'

Spud and Star sat up straight and looked amazed. *What! Us? What did we do? We were on our way home on the train!*

Lara smiled to herself.

'When the pups first went to check out Stanley Strange that night, they took a tracking device with them,' said the professor.

*Yes, that's right, the one we were going to fix on the car!* thought Spud.

'In the confusion, they must have dropped it into one of the Santa Claus boots. Strange lost one to Lara,' smiled the professor. 'But luckily the tracker was in his other boot and he kept it on the whole time. We were able to track his every move! So when he got to the airport, it wasn't just that jet there waiting for him – Special Branch was there as well!'

The pups' eyes grew wide with astonishment. They had caught the baddie after all!

'Incredible!' said Ben. 'Nice work, pups!'

'Yes,' said Sophie. 'But what happened to the money?'

'It's all gone straight back to the shop,' said the professor. 'Apart from this cheque that the manager asked me to give to Lara and the pups by way of a reward.'

He waved the cheque in the air. Lara glanced at it and the pups peered over her shoulder. *It's far too much – we were only doing our duty!*

'But Lara says she and the pups already have everything they could wish for,' said the professor, waving his hand around the room.

*That's right*, thought Lara. *Family, friends, oodles of Christmas presents, good health – apart from my broken ribs, and I'm sure they'll soon be better.*

'So – ,' went on the professor. 'Oh, I say, this

bread sauce is scrumptious, Mrs Cook! May I have a little more?'

Sophie passed the professor the bread sauce, and everyone waited while he poured some on the side of his plate.

'As I was saying,' he continued at last, 'Lara thinks that, as Stanley Strange wouldn't give anything to the carol singers that night, up at End House – it would be a nice idea to give the reward money to the children's charity on his behalf.'

'That's a wonderful idea!' said Mum, giving Lara a hug. 'Oh, sorry,' she said as the family pet couldn't help wincing.

'Good for you, Lara!' agreed Dad. 'And well done, you pups, for agreeing to it.'

*Well, we didn't exactly agree . . .* thought Spud.

*It's the first we've heard about it . . .* thought Star.

*But, yes, we think it's a great idea!* And they both wagged their tails happily and tucked into another sausage.

'Well, Merry Christmas!' said Mum, smiling round the table. 'And do you think it would be too much for me to hope for a peaceful, *non-eventful* New Year?'

'Only time will tell, Mrs Cook,' laughed the professor. 'But let's hope for a very happy one at least! Merry Christmas, everyone!'

Turn the page for a sneak peek from . . .

# SPY PUPS

## TREASURE QUEST

## 1. Double Trouble

'Don't be sad, Lara,' soothed Ollie, stroking his dog behind the ear. 'You've still got two puppies left and Mum says we can keep them.'

'And the others have gone to brilliant homes,' added Sophie, trying but failing to sound chirpy.

Lara lay with her head on her paws. She knew the children were right but it didn't stop the pain in her heart. *Hopefully time will heal it*, she thought. *It's so difficult when my babies leave home.* She watched Spud and Star play-fighting. *Bags of energy*, she thought. 'Calm down, you two,' she woofed. 'Why don't you play Scrabble or Monopoly or something a bit calmer?' Her two remaining puppies looked at their mum as if she was mad. Chasing each other around the lounge was much more fun.

Lara reflected on the last four months. *It's been a hectic time*, she smiled. *Becoming a mum of seven, instilling some discipline, getting the pups house-trained and teaching them some of the spy-dog basics. Phew! No wonder I'm always exhausted.*

Lara watched as Spud sat on his sister, squeezing the breath out of her.

'Gotcha!' he barked.

'No, you haven't,' she woofed, twisting away and nipping him on the backside. 'Too slow, bro!'

Lara always knew that most of the pups would be adopted. Dad had explained it to her shortly after she found she was pregnant. And Lara understood – the house just wasn't big enough to keep them all. Her mission was to find good homes. Each time there was an adoption her tummy churned with happiness and sadness. She was delighted with the new owners. Her eldest daughter, Bessie, had gone to a farmer. He had other dogs and Lara knew they were well cared for. Bessie had a good life ahead of her as a working farm dog. *Perfect*, thought the retired spy dog. *One sorted, seven to go!*

Toddy and Mr G had gone as a pair, hand selected by the police as sniffer dogs. Lara approved. *They are both lively boys*, she thought, *so they will get all the action they crave. And maybe do some good for the world too.* Lara reflected on her spy-dog days and shuddered at the thought of all the baddies she'd stopped, especially her arch-enemy, Mr Big. *I sniffed out his evil drugs empire and put him behind bars.*

*Twice! Maybe my boys will do the same*, she hoped.

Lara had a particular soft spot for Britney. She was the youngest – *a whole nineteen minutes younger than Bessie* – and quietest of the litter. *Seen but not heard*, thought Lara. *Definitely not police dog material but very clever and a great companion. Being selected as a guide dog was perfect*, reflected Lara. *She'll be the top of her class and there will be one very lucky owner!*

TinTin was always going to be a handful. He was a rather strange-looking pup. His brothers and sisters were black and white but TinTin was splodged with brown patches. His energy levels were off the scale and his tail never stopped wagging. He was sometimes a little overenthusiastic. His shaggy coat made him the perfect choice to go and work with his granddad, Leo, in Scotland. TinTin had enrolled to be a mountain rescue dog and his mum couldn't be more proud. *A very worthwhile career. And I know his granddad will take good care of him.*

Lara watched her two remaining puppies chasing around the table legs. *Good homes, all*

*of them*, she thought. *And I'm lucky that the Cook family have let me keep these two.*

'Mum, what's for lunch?' asked Spud, taking a break from annoying his sister.

Lara sniffed the air. 'Spaghetti hoops ... peas,' she woofed, '... and sausages.'

'And when's it lunchtime?' yapped her son. 'I'm starving.'

'You're always starving!' Lara glanced at the clock. 'Half an hour,' she replied.

'How long's half an hour?' asked Spud.

'Not long,' she barked, rising wearily to her feet and stretching. 'Just long enough to work on those times tables before we eat!'

## 2. Cat Burglar

Lunch was cleared away and it was time for the pups' afternoon snooze. Lara loved living with the Cooks. *It's not all out adventure and excitement like when I was a spy dog,* she thought, *but we've certainly had more than our fair share of scrapes.*

Lara had adopted the Cooks when they'd turned up at the RSPCA. Before then she'd been working as a spy dog for the Secret Service – the name LARA on her tag actually stood for 'Licensed Assault and Rescue Animal'. But one of her spy-dog missions had gone horribly wrong and her orders were clear. *I was to give myself up to the nearest dog rescue shelter and then adopt a family and wait for help. And I couldn't have chosen better,* she smiled, looking around the room at the

Cook children. Ollie had Spud on his knee. The puppy was fast asleep, snoring gently, his chubby tummy breathing in and out. Ollie was the youngest of the children and Lara loved his playfulness. Star and Spud adored him too. Lara watched as Star leapt on to Ollie's lap and snuggled down for an afternoon snooze.

Sophie couldn't help but wander over to her brother and stroke the pups. 'They're sooo cute,' she purred. 'And so squidgy!' Sophie was a true animal lover, destined to become a vet. A chinchilla had been top of her Christmas list for three years running. 'It's a house, not a bloomin' zoo,' was her dad's favourite comment. He always told Sophie she could have a chinchilla if they traded Lara in exchange. He knew there was no way that would ever happen.

Ben was the eldest and therefore the leader. Although Lara was officially the family pet, he regarded her as *his* dog. The pair would spend hours fishing at the canal or playing football in the garden. Star and Spud were a bit young but had begun to practise their headers and volleys. Star could do forty keepie-uppies and Spud had perfected his goal-scoring celebration – a backflip like he'd seen on TV. It was exhausting and they always needed their long afternoon sleeps!

'I think Star will be a good footballer,' Ben told Lara. 'She's got your natural ability.'

Lara looked across at the sleeping Star. She was a tiny puppy with one sticky-up ear just like her mum. She also had the same trademark black and white splodges, including a patch over her eye. She had tiny razor teeth and a very long tongue that sometimes peeped out when she was asleep. *And so clever!*

Lara watched as Spud woke and wandered over to the games console. *Just puppy fat, I'm sure*, she thought, smiling at his low-hanging belly. Spud was bigger than his sister. *Probably because of his liking for custard creams*, thought Lara. A guilty thought passed through her mind. *I wonder where he gets that from!* Spud was a handsome dog, like his father, Potter. Spud had a shiny black coat and a playful puppy face. His ears were a matching pair: floppy, except when he was concentrating or when someone mentioned food. Then he had the biggest ears in the world, pricked and listening for scrapings into his bowl. *Not quite as bright as his sister*, she considered, *although the BrainBox training game is doing him some good.*

Lara was pleased the building work at home had finished. At first she'd been reluctant when the Secret Service had suggested a security upgrade. But Professor Cortex had been very persuasive, arguing that it would allow her to improve the pet neighbourhood watch scheme that she'd set up.

'And now you're a mother,' the professor frowned, 'you have to be extra careful of enemy agents.'

Lara's office was now complete. She pressed the button with her nose and stood in front of the fireplace. *3 . . . 2 . . . 1 . . .*, she counted, and the hearth moved, rotating Lara into her secret office. She sat at the laptop and fixed her spectacles on the end of her nose. Lara took a pencil in her mouth and logged on to her emails. *Nothing particularly exciting*, she thought, although she was pleased to see a message from Professor Cortex confirming tomorrow's visit to Spy School. *Star and Spud will love it*, she thought. *The professor always has oodles of new gadgets and whacky ideas.*

Lara loved the professor. He was a bit grumpy on the outside but a great big softie on the inside. *He was the one who trained me as a spy dog. And who gave me that ridiculous code name, GM451. I am so pleased the family have chosen to call me by my other code name.*

Lara clicked a remote control and various CCTV camera pictures were beamed on to the screen in front of her. She could see most of the neighbourhood from here. The professor's voice replayed in her head. 'You can never be too careful, GM451. You are the cleverest animal in the world. No other animal can understand every human word. Or defuse a bomb. Or play chess, for that matter.' *And he should know*, thought Lara. *He's head of Spy School. And probably the cleverest, maddest scientist in the world.* Lara couldn't quite see where the danger would come from. *After all, this is a quiet road and*

*I'm retired from active spy-dog service,* she thought. *I can't see that any more baddies are going to come looking for me. But this office is cool,* she admitted, spinning herself round on her leather chair. She cast her mind back over the last year. *Not quite the retirement I'd planned. So many adventures!* Lara shuddered as she remembered falling off a space rocket as it took off, and stopping a diamond robbery. *But being a mum definitely changes things. This time I've given up for real. From now on it's the quiet life for me and the pups.*

Lara watched on CCTV as Mr Granger from number 42 tipped his grass cuttings into next door's garden. *They won't be happy,* she thought. Through another camera she saw a delivery van pull up at number 7. *New sofa,* she noted. *And what a nice pattern.*

*Nothing suspicious,* she thought. *No sign of baddies.* Lara zoomed in to the van parked outside number 22. *Window cleaner,* she read. *New bloke, by the look of it.* Lara watched for a minute. The man climbed the ladder and she watched with interest as he looked all around before reaching into the upstairs window and climbing in. *Er, I don't think he should be doing that*, she thought, zooming closer still until she could see through the open window. The CCTV showed the window cleaner snooping around the bedroom, putting trinkets into a bag. Suddenly, Lara was on full alert. She looked at her map of the close. *Number 22, Mr and Mrs Winslow. Both teachers. Both out at work all day! Yikes, I think this is a robbery!*

# Spy Pups Family Fact File

**Name:** Laika
**Nationality:** Russian
The first dog in space, Laika was always thought to have died in orbit, but can it really be coincidence that GM451 has the very same silly ears and superbrain?

**Name**: Leo
**Nationality**: Scottish
Once strong as an ox, Leo is getting old these days, but it doesn't stop him from using determination to save Lara – and the day!

**Name:** Lara (Licensed Assault and Rescue Animal)
**Nationality:** British
The original Spy Dog! Skills include: karate, languages, typing with a pencil, driving cars, leadership – and more!

**Name:** Potter
**Nationality:** British
Lara's second in command, Potter is a good all-rounder: a sympathetic, intelligent dog with a positive attitude.

# Bright and shiny and sizzling with fun stuff . . .

# puffin.co.uk

### WEB FUN

**UNIQUE and exclusive digital content!**
Podcasts, photos, Q&A, Day in the Life of, interviews
and much more, from Eoin Colfer, Cathy Cassidy,
Allan Ahlberg and Meg Rosoff to Lynley Dodd!

### WEB NEWS

The **Puffin Blog** is packed with posts and photos from
Puffin HQ and special guest bloggers. You can also sign up
to our monthly newsletter **Puffin Beak Speak**

### WEB CHAT

**Discover something new** EVERY month –
books, competitions and treats galore

### WEBBED FEET

(Puffins have funny little feet and
brightly coloured beaks)

## Point your mouse our way today!

# It all started with a Scarecrow.

**Puffin is seventy years old.**
Sounds ancient, doesn't it? But Puffin has never been
so lively. We're always on the lookout for the next big
idea, which is how it began all those years ago.

Penguin Books was a big idea from the mind of
a man called Allen Lane, who in 1935 invented
the quality paperback and changed the world.
**And from great Penguins, great Puffins grew,
changing the face of children's books forever.**

The first four Puffin Picture Books were hatched in 1940 and the
first Puffin story book featured a man with broomstick arms called
Worzel Gummidge. In 1967 Kaye Webb, Puffin Editor, started the
Puffin Club, promising to **'make children into readers'**.
She kept that promise and over 200,000 children became
devoted Puffineers through their quarterly instalments of
*Puffin Post*, which is now back for a new generation.

Many years from now, we hope you'll look back and
remember Puffin with a smile. **No matter what your age
or what you're into, there's a Puffin for everyone.**
The possibilities are endless, but one thing is for sure:
whether it's a picture book or a paperback, a sticker book
or a hardback, **if it's got that little Puffin
on it – it's bound to be good.**